Put it on the Pizza!

T03337141

Written by Jane Clarke

Illustrated by Elisa Rocchi

Collins

Who's in this story?

Listen and say

Tim

Tess

Download the audio at www.collins.co.uk/839685

Dad

Tess and Tim want to make pizza.

Tim says, "Let's put *ten* tomatoes on it."

Tess asks, "Would you like any mushrooms on the pizza?"

Tim asks, "Would you like any onions on it?"

Yuck! **NO** onions!

Tess says, "Would you like any pineapple on the pizza?"

Tim says, "Let's put *six* bits of pineapple on the pizza."

Yum! I love fruit on pizza!

9

Tim says, "Yes, fruit is great on pizza!"
Tess says, "Look! There's lots of fruit in the fruit bowl."

Tess says, "There are eight grapes. Four for you and four for me."

Tim says, "Correct! Put them on the pizza!"

Tim says, "There's one banana. Let's put it on the pizza!"

Tess says, "Hmm ... I like biscuits.
Let's put some biscuits on the pizza, too!"

Tess says, "Wow! Marshmallows! Count them out!"

Tim says, "Nine for you and nine for me!"

Tim says, "Tomatoes, pineapple, grapes, banana, biscuits and marshmallows."

Tim asks, "How about some cereal?"

Tess says, "Yum! I love cereal. Put some on the pizza!"

Tess says, "Wow! There's lots of cereal!"

Tess says, "And lots of cheese. Yum!"
Tim says, "Let's cook the pizza, Dad!"

Dad says, "OK."

Dad asks, "Would you like some salad?"

Picture dictionary

Listen and repeat

banana

biscuit

cereal

cheese

grapes

marshmallow

mushrooms

onion

pineapple

pizza

tomato

1 Look and order the story

2 Listen and say

Collins

Published by Collins
An imprint of HarperCollins*Publishers*
Westerhill Road
Bishopbriggs
Glasgow
G64 2QT

HarperCollins*Publishers*
1st Floor, Watermarque Building
Ringsend Road
Dublin 4
Ireland

William Collins' dream of knowledge for all began with the publication of his first book in 1819.

A self-educated mill worker, he not only enriched millions of lives, but also founded a flourishing publishing house. Today, staying true to this spirit, Collins books are packed with inspiration, innovation and practical expertise. They place you at the centre of a world of possibility and give you exactly what you need to explore it.

© HarperCollins*Publishers* Limited 2020

10 9 8 7 6 5 4 3 2

ISBN 978-0-00-839685-5

Collins® and COBUILD® are registered trademarks of HarperCollins*Publishers* Limited

www.collins.co.uk/elt

British Library Cataloguing in Publication Data

A catalogue record for this publication is available from the British Library.

Author: Jane Clarke
Illustrator: Elisa Rocchi (Beehive)
Series editor: Rebecca Adlard
Publishing manager: Lisa Todd
Product managers: Jennifer Hall and Caroline Green
In-house editor: Alma Puts Keren
Project manager: Emily Hooton
Editor: Rebecca Adlard
Proofreaders: Natalie Murray and Michael Lamb
Cover designer: Kevin Robbins
Typesetter: 2Hoots Publishing Services Ltd
Audio produced by id audio, London
Reading guide author: Katie Foufouti
Production controller: Rachel Weaver
Printed and bound by: GPS Group, Slovenia

MIX
Paper from responsible sources

FSC
www.fsc.org

FSC™ C007454

This book is produced from independently certified FSC™ paper to ensure responsible forest management.

For more information visit: **www.harpercollins.co.uk/green**

Download the audio for this book and a reading guide for parents and teachers at www.collins.co.uk/839685